THIS ORCHARD BOOK

BELONGS TO:

....

For Guy Brendan - M.R.

For Theo - L.L.

ORCHARD BOOKS

338 Euston Road, London NW1 3BH

Orchard Books Australia Level 17/207 Kent Street, Sydney, NSW 2000

First published in 2013 by Orchard Books

First published in paperback in 2013 ISBN 978 1 40831 201 8

Text © Michelle Robinson 2013 Illustrations © Leonie Lord 2013

The rights of Michelle Robinson to be identified as the author and of Leonie Lord to be identified as the illustrator

of this book have been asserted by them in accordance with the Copyright, Designs and Patents Act, 1988.

A CIP catalogue record for this book is available from the British Library.

1 3 5 7 9 10 8 6 4 2

Printed in China

Orchard Books is a division of Hachette Children's Books,

an Hachette UK company.

www.hachette.co.uk

DING DONG GORILLA!

MICHELLE ROBINSON   LEONIE LORD

ORCHARD

You know we ordered a pizza?

A GREAT **BIG**

ONE WITH **EXTRA** CHEESE?

Well, I'm afraid I have some BAD news ...

YOU SEE, while you were upstairs, getting ready for dinner, the doorbell rang.

DING DONG!

I thought it must be the pizza boy, so I answered it.

DIAL A PIZZA

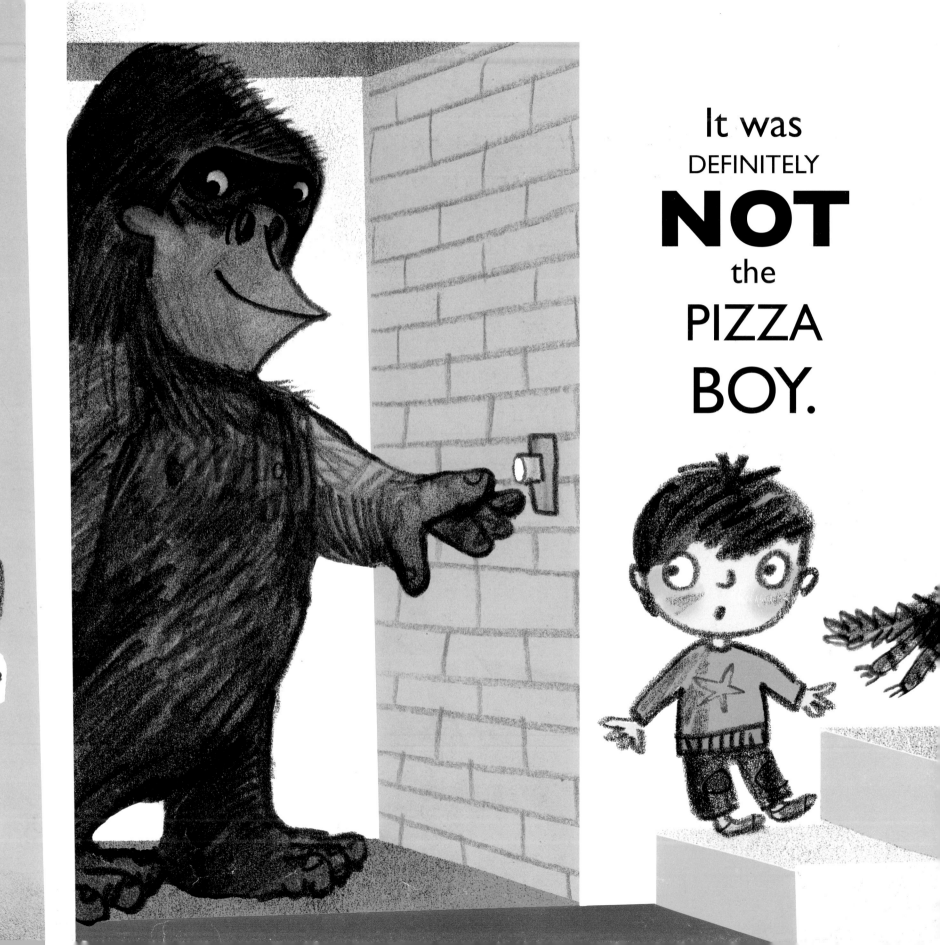

It was
DEFINITELY
NOT
the
PIZZA
BOY.

I didn't invite the gorilla in, he just barged past me.

He went straight to my **TOY BOX** and tipped everything out to get at the CRAYONS.

He did LOTS of **COLOURING IN,** but he wasn't very good at staying between the lines.

But that's not the **BAD** NEWS...

When the gorilla got bored he
STOMPED OFF
to watch TV.

He went through all my movies, but at least he put them away afterwards.

JUST NOT IN THE RIGHT PLACES...

That's not the BAD news, either.

Next, the gorilla wanted
to play dressing up.

**I COULDN'T
STOP HIM!**

He put on all my
clothes (and most
of yours, too).

THEN
HE LEFT
THEM IN A
DIRTY HEAP
ON MY BEDROOM FLOOR.

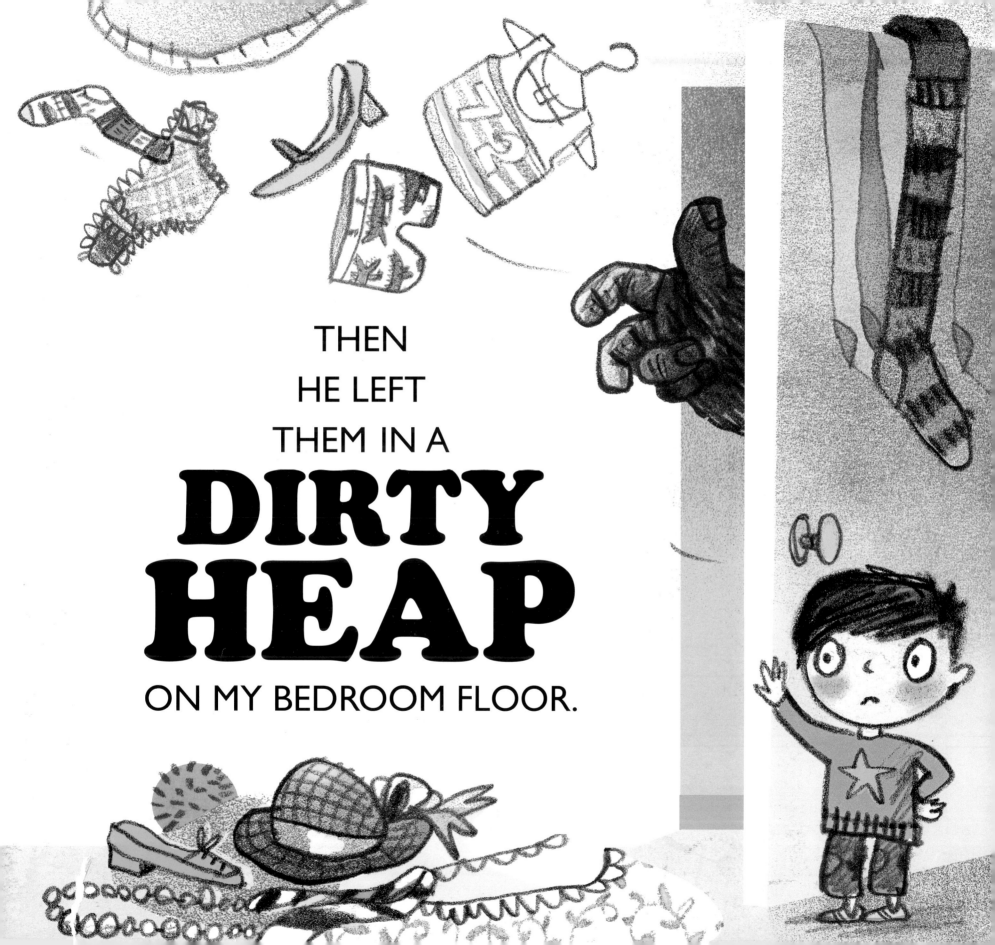

But
even that's
not such
bad news,

because
at least he
washed

SOME
of

them.

I thought perhaps the gorilla was over-excited,
so I sent him outside to get some fresh air...

...but he got some fresh flowers instead.
The garden doesn't look so pretty anymore...

The gorilla wanted to play

FOOTBALL

next, but it was getting
a bit dark.

So we came
back inside.

It wasn't me
who broke the

VASE...

or the
WINDOW...

or the **chair**...

And that STILL
isn't the BAD news...

By now the gorilla was GETTING REALLY **HUNGRY**. I was a bit scared, but he wasn't interested in me.

He wanted to bake a **CHOCOLATE CAKE**.

THIS TIME IT
REALLY
WAS
the
PIZZA
BOY.

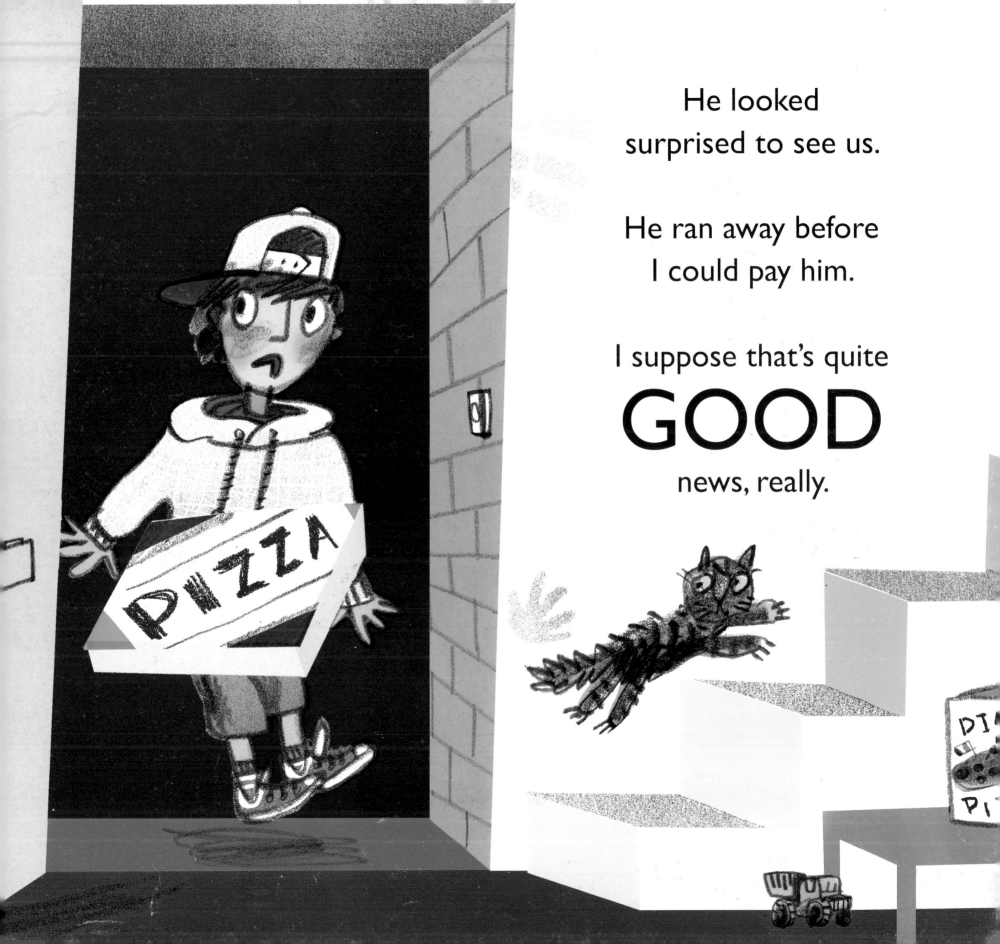

He looked
surprised to see us.

He ran away before
I could pay him.

I suppose that's quite

GOOD

news, really.

But the gorilla ran away when he heard you coming downstairs.

So you probably won't believe that HE made all this mess.

You are BOUND to blame me and send me to bed without any pizza.

But the
BAD
news is…